Fire Drops

Ricardo Castillo

www.rEEpublishing,.com

Fire Drops

ISBN: 978-1-7354321-0-6 (hardcover)
ISBN: 978-1-7354321-1-3 (paperback)
ISBN: 978-1-7354321-2-0 (ebook)

The characters found in this book are fictional. Any similarity to real life people is purely coincidental.

Editors: Brian Saliba, Taylor Morris, Joel Pierson, and Trevor Courneen
Cover design by: Rebeca-Ira P. and Ricardo Castillo
Illustrations by: Ricardo Castillo

Published by:
rEEcreation, LLC
18117 Biscayne Boulevard, Ste. 2141
Aventura, Florida 33160
www.rEEpublishing.com

Library of Congress Control Number: 2020913275

Names: Castillo, Ricardo, 1978- author, illustrator.
Title: Fire drops / Ricardo Castillo.
Description: Aventura, Florida : rEE Creation, LLC, [2020] | Audience: Grades 4th through 9th. | Summary: "Fire Drops" is a fiction story for children about water droplets whose memories have been compromised. Water droplets do not remember who they are and must find their way to answers no one seems to have. To discover who they truly are, water droplets must come together, embrace their surroundings, accept their limitations, and free their minds to defy preconceived notions of hate and fear. Fire Drops parallels the human condition in that, when we are born, we have no memories, and every human being must journey through life to discover self-identity and purpose. Fire Drops is a celebration of life-- the most awe-provoking force in the universe.--Publisher.
Identifiers: ISBN: 978-1-7354321-0-6 (hardcover) | 978-1-7354321-1-3 (paperback) | 978-1-7354321-2-0 (ebook) | LCCN: 2020913275
Subjects: LCSH: Water--Juvenile fiction. | Fire--Juvenile fiction. | Memory in infants--Juvenile fiction. | Memory in children--Juvenile fiction. | Identity (Psychology) in children--Juvenile fiction. | Prejudices in children--Prevention--Juvenile fiction. | Toleration--Juvenile fiction. | Self-perception--Juvenile fiction. | Self-realization--Juvenile fiction. | Self-actualization (Psychology) in children--Juvenile fiction. | Self-actualization (Psychology) in adolescence--Juvenile fiction. | Children--Conduct of life. | Youth--Conduct of life. | CYAC: Water--Fiction. | Fire--Fiction. | Memory--Fiction. | Identity--Fiction. | Prejudices--Prevention--Fiction. | Toleration--Fiction. | Self-perception--Fiction. | Self-realization--Fiction. | Self-actualization (Psychology)--Fiction. | Conduct of life--Fiction.
Classification: LCC: PZ7.1.C447 F57 2020 | DDC: [Fic]--dc23

Fire Drops is dedicated to
the spirit of life in all of us.

"Mind you, there is no such thing as death,
for death is merely life in disguise." —Abidemi

CONTENTS

CONTENTS

- Scene 1 -

Base hit. Pitico whistles his signature low-to-high toot as he slides into second base and picks up layers of dust on his already grimy and torn jeans. He looks back to first; Ragmouth made it. He turns around and sees Omar, who is still on third. Things could not be better—the bases are loaded, and Rosa, the next batter, is the perfect ringer. Her hand-to-eye coordination is amazing, and she can bat in any direction she wishes. On her way to home plate, Rosa picks up the bat and holds it up in the air so that everyone can see. The only bat the children have is broken. Ragmouth had unintentionally scraped the ground with it during his last swing, causing the wood to crack. No bat means no game, and therefore, they will have to finish the game some other time, whenever someone finds a new one.

Pitico looks at his clothes and starts dusting off his jeans with the palms of his hands. Every pat on his jeans releases puffs of dust that rise to the air like smoke from a smothered campfire. The wind carries the puffs away to settle elsewhere, but the tiniest of the particles don't settle. Instead, they are carried up by the wind to a height of about ten kilometers into the Earth's atmosphere. This atmospheric layer is called the *troposphere*, and it is where rainclouds form. After water evaporates from oceans, rivers, and everywhere from the surface of the Earth, minuscule water molecules in the form of vapor elevate to the troposphere. At this height, the molecules are moving fast—so fast they cannot cling to one another to form drops that are big enough to rain down. However, dust particles in the troposphere, including the very same dust particles from Pitico's clothes, are the perfect vehicle for water vapor to condense. The first water molecule to condense contains the essence, the core of a drop's personality. Any other molecule joining thereafter simply adds volume to it. Normally, the more moisture that is available in the troposphere, the bigger the raindrops become.

Early the next morning, Soet, a newly formed raindrop, rains over La Hispaniola. To his left, a massive water droplet called Vis shouts a few words to Soet, but the loud whooshing winds in the clouds make communication nearly impossible.

"What?" Soet calls loudly.

"I said, hello," Vis responds.

"Oh, hi there. Where——where are we? What are we doing here?"

Vis answers, "You's like every other drop I spoke to——when they done wakin' up, don't know a thing. I tell you what—we been here for a long, long while."

"Well, someone must know *something!*" Soet says.

"No one knows nothin' except——"

Soet prompts him. "Except?"

Vis's silent stare into the distance invites Soet to look up ahead. "What is that?" Soet asks.

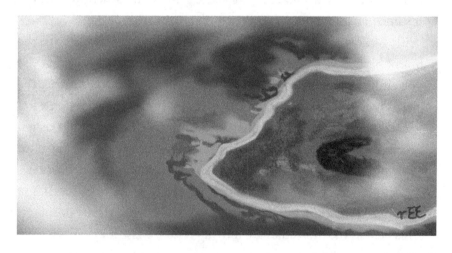

"No one knows nothin'."

Right below them, a tropical greenery surrounded by a turquoise Caribbean Sea appears as two inescapable realities: if the raindrops steer to the left, they will drop into the ocean, but if they steer to the right, they will fall right on land.

"What do we do?" Soet asks.

"I'd love to answer, um ..." Vis says in response, inviting Soet to give his name.

"Soet. I'm Soet."

"Well, Soet, all this here is Vis. I ain't got the slightest idea what to do, but blue's my favorite color. You's go ahead and drop on green and find me in the middle. That way, we might be able to get some answers."

"What?" Soet asks, now very confused.

Flying away, Vis says, "Just go green. Find Vis in the middle!"

"Okay," Soet mutters to himself, "I can do that. Go green; find Vis in the middle."

The wind allows both companions to maneuver themselves through the sky. As agreed, Vis accelerates to the left, in the direction of the blue region in front of him. Soon enough, the anticipated blue comes into focus, and Vis is mesmerized by its back-and-forth movement, to and from the green area. Little by little, he begins to see millions upon millions of faces. The blue region, though it appears to be a single body in motion at first sight, is really a vast number of individual droplets just like him!

Life comes assorted in different-sized adventures for anyone who grows up in Miches. Like clockwork, at six thirty in the morning, the milkman begins his rounds throughout town. His young ox, Fifa, pulls a wooden wagon with five tanks filled with milk. Fifa is rather an unusual name for a male, but the kids who named him did so without knowing the difference between an ox and a milk cow. The bell around his neck announces their arrival, marking this one of the first morning sights for most people. Whoever wants fresh milk comes out of their homes with pots to purchase one or two gallons for fifty cheles each, and for the same price, the children of Miches

get to pet Fifa. The milkman fills the pots while his wife collects payment. In a short time, all transactions are completed, and Fifa bids his farewell to the children by wagging his tail. Then the children run inside to prepare for school, and by the time they are ready, loaves of bread with butter and a glass of boiled milk mixed with cocoa powder are usually placed on the table for breakfast.

By no means does Pitico consider school to be hard. He is now ten and understands the benefits of being able to read and to play with numbers. *Matemáticas*

is what his teacher calls it. His parents were not fortunate enough to learn how to read when they themselves were children. They had to help their parents run the family farm, which was an endless task that left no time for schooling. However, Pitico's parents grew up to be successful business owners. His mom, Clara, is gifted with needle and thread. She makes alterations to garments for just about everyone in town, and his dad, Braulio, is a woodcrafter. He can build nearly anything out of wood in his shop.

School is out right on time for lunch, and one of the best parts of the day is coming home to eat. The food itself is never a mystery: coconut rice with beans, either a slice of avocado or some fried sweet plantains called *maduros*, and some type of sautéed bird. Mom makes it so good that Pitico wouldn't want to eat anything else, no matter how many times the same food is cooked for him.

While eating at the lunch table, they often laugh and tell jokes about the day's occurrences. Today, for example, Pitico's dad had to fire Manolo, an eighteen-year-old woodshop apprentice who had been recommended by Clara's sister, Teresa. Because the recommendation had come from Teresa, Clara had taken a special interest in Manolo's success.

"¿Cómo 'tuvo Manolo hoy?" Clara asks. [How did Manolo do today?]

"Que va. Tuve que botarlo," Braulio answers. [Not good. I had to let him go.]

"¡Que! No-no-no. Tu tiene' que darle una oportunida' a ese mucha-cho. Mira que Tere me dice que él e' bien bueno, vaya, una persona que se sienta y analiza muy bien to' lo tu le dice'." [What! No-no-no. You have to give that kid a chance. Tere tells me he's the type of person who sits down and analyzes what he's being told.]

"Bueno," Braulio says, "yo traté y resulta que la carpintería no e' pa' to' el mundo, Clara." [I tried, Clara, but it turns out woodshop's not for everyone.]

Pitico asks, "¿Qué fue lo que pasó papi?" [What happened, Daddy?]

Braulio answers, "Ma' bien, qué fue lo que no pasó. E'tabamo' en parte de atrá, donde se barniza la madera y le digo, 'Buen día, Manolo. Hoy tenemo' que ternima' una mesa con sei' silla'. Dale una lijita a la mesa en lo que yo barnizo la' silla'.' ¿Y tu sabe' lo que hizo?" [Better yet, what didn't happen? We're out in the back, where I stain the wood, and I tell him, "Good mornin' Manolo. We've got to finish a table and six chairs by noon today. Please sand the table a little bit while I stain the chairs." And you know what he did?]

"¿Qué hizo?" Clara asks. [What?]

"Parece que se emocionó y lijó una pata demasiado. Ahora la mesa tiene tre' pata gorda y una flaca." [I guess he got too excited and sanded one of the legs way too much. Now the table has three fat legs and a skinny one.]

Pitico laughs. "¡Eso e' una mesa pirata, papi! Ah Ja-ja-ja!" [Daddy, that's a pirate table! Ah ha-ha-ha!]

"Ay Dio' mio," Clara says. "¿Y entoce'?" [Good Lor'. And then?]

"Na'. Como tu diji'te. Manolo se sentó pa' analiza' la cosa," Braulio says. [Nothin'. Like you said. Manolo sat down to analyze what had happened.]

Clara smiles. "Si. Él e' así." [Yep. That's Manolo alrigh'.]

"Ta' bien, pero se me sentó en la silla que yo acaba de barnizá'." [And that's alrigh' with me, but he sat on the chair that I had just finished staining.]

Pitico laughs at the mental image.

Clara begins to wonder. "¿Tu me 'ta' diciendo la verda'?" [Is this a true story?]

Braulio smiles. He knows he's caught. "No."

They all start laughing uncontrollably and, in between laughter, Braulio reassures Clara that Manolo is a fine apprentice.

It is usually at the lunch table where the children of Miches negotiate their parents' permission to play *bitilla* with the rest of the kids in the neighborhood. Bitilla (pronounced bee-tee-yah) is not only the name of the game but also what they call the caps taken from five-gallon water bottles. This game is identical to baseball, with the exception that kids use those bottle caps as balls and broomsticks as bats because of lack of resources.

A bitilla cuts through the air like a Frisbee, but being smaller than a Frisbee, it flies considerably faster and changes direction sharply. The kids enjoy this game, but there are consequences for losing. The losing team is responsible for bringing a bat from home to the next game. This is a daunting task because it means having to "borrow" a broomstick from annoyed parents who have often swept their floors with broken brooms. Indeed, for every bitilla game in progress, there is at least one aggravated parent wondering how to sweep the floor without bent backs.

Pitico asks, "¿Papi, puedo i' a juga' Bitilla depue' que coma?" [Daddy, can I play bitilla after lunch?]

"¡A Dio' pero tú nunca falla con eso! Ayer te dije lo mi'mo y antier te he dicho lo mi'mo. Señor, coma su comida tranquilo y de'pue' haga su tarea." [Good Lor', this is an everyday ordeal with you, boy! I keep telling you the same thing: eat your food and then do your homework.]

"Mi'jo no e' bueno que coma' y depue' te ponga a brinca' como un chivo porai," Clara reminds him. [Jumpin' like a goat after eating won't do you any good neither, son.]

"Pero déjenme i' que hoy no me dejan' tarea, y Boca-e-trapo me va a esta' e'perando." [Well, I didn't get any homework today, so can I go? Look, Ragmouth's counting on me.]

Braulio decides to allow it. "Bueno, bueno ... no me deje ni un solo granito de arró' en el plato. Dale un beso a tu mai, y pasa por el taller ante' de i'te. ¡Ah y cuidao' con coger el palo de la e'coba!" [All right, all right ... don't leave a single grain of rice on your plate. Give your mom a kiss before you leave, and come by the shop before you go to the field. Ah, and don't take the broomstick!]

In no time, Pitico devours his meal, carefully making sure that not a single grain of rice is left on his plate. Clara observes him and smiles.

"Bebe much'agua mi'jo. Mira que sin agua no somos nada." [Drink a lot of water, son—we're mostly water, you know.]

Pitico swallows the last grains in his mouth and follows them with a loud gulp of water. He quickly gets up to kiss his mom and runs to his room to change into the most raggedy clothes he can find. Still at the table, Braulio looks at Clara lovingly, reaches across, and takes her hands. It is his way of thanking her for the meal. His rugged hands are coarse enough to sand rocks to a shine, but since Clara's hands have also suffered their fair share of pricks and cuts from sewing, his touch feels more like feathers to her. Braulio gets up from the table and grunts while stretching his back from side to side. He grabs his hat and heads back to the shop.

The woodshop is by the riverbank, which is merely half a kilometer away from home. This is often a nice walk for Braulio, who enjoys small talk with his neighbors. Down the winding path, Braulio comes across Chencha's home. She's crouching with broom in hand and attempting to sweep her front porch. He calls out to her.

"Hola, mi Doña." [Hello there.]

Chencha looks up and wipes the sweat off her brow with her forearm. She says, "Don Braulio. Cria' muchacho no e' fácil." [Hello, Braulio. I tell you something—child rearing ain't for the faint of heart.]

He smiles. "U'te' lo dice y no lo cree." [It sure ain't.]

They both laugh, and Braulio continues his walk. Soon after he arrives at the shop, Braulio sees Pitico a few steps behind him. "Llega'te volando," he says in surprise. [You flew over here.]

Braulio unlocks the door and walks past the customer counter, toward the back of the shop. Pitico follows him closely. To Pitico's eyes, the back of the shop seems enormous. There are shelves that run from the floor to the ceiling along all the walls. Braulio groups and stores the same species of wood on these shelves. Right in the middle of the room, there is also a large workbench where Braulio does the carpentry. He walks toward the bench and grabs a rectangular case.

"Mira, ábrelo," Braulio says. [Here, open it.]

Inside the case is a wooden bat Braulio crafted for Pitico. A few weeks earlier, Braulio had noticed that Pitico was at a disadvantage when using the "bat" the bigger kids brought with them to the field. Braulio determines that although there is no money for a new bat, one can be crafted out of leftover wood laying around the shop. Pitico holds the bat in his hands, examines it, and smiles, causing Braulio to sprout a smile. The bat is strong, not too light and not too heavy, with "Pitico" inscribed along the side. It is perfect. "Phwwee-phwwoo," Pitico whistles.

He thanks his dad and runs to the field with this new bat. As he runs, he looks at the sky and sees that a few clouds have gathered since the morning. *Man! It looks like rain. I'll tie up a rock as soon as I make it,* he thinks to himself. When done right, the children believe this trick drives the rain away.

- Scene 3 -

As agreed, Soet steers to the right into the thickest part of the greenery. Upon reaching the ground, he crashes onto the leaves of an old mango tree. Each collision with each leaf helps break his fall until reaching a final leaf, where he splatters into smaller parts. The leaf's age has curved its brown and dry texture inward, allowing gravity to gradually join each of his parts back together at the leaf's midrib. He becomes whole again.

Gravity drags Soet to the leaf's tip, where he dangles for a moment before dropping onto a half-pecked mango that hangs from a brittle branch. Resting belly-up and sliding to the edge of the mango peel, Soet opens his eyes and finds himself surrounded by the massive shades of numerous cedars, calabash, and mahogany trees that block much of the blue skies from which he came. He slides down to the very end of the peel, but on his way down, absorbs much of the stickiness of the fruit and now hangs motionless in midair. A voice calls out from the ground, "Come on now, keep pushing. You can do it."

Soet manages to overcome the glueyness of the fruit to look down at the ground. After scanning the soil beneath for a few seconds, he finds a group of droplets attentively looking back at him. In front of them is Nia, a droplet who has managed to remain clean water despite many encountered perils.

Soet takes a deep breath and pushes himself off the mango peel with all his might. Despite his effort, however, he manages to slither only a little bit. The mango's gooiness has engulfed him so much that his appearance is no longer transparent but orange like a ripe mango. Still determined, he realizes that pushing himself off does not work, so he begins to swing from side to side. The mango's drool becomes elongated with every swing, and although Soet is far off the ground, he makes a slow and safe descent, landing gently on the ground.

"Well done!" Nia says. "We would have loved to climb up and help you down, but you know ... we like traveling down. Let me guess—you just came from above, didn't you?"

"Yes. A whole bunch of us rained down at once."

"Hmm, and where do you think you are?" Nia asks.

"I don't know."

"But you know you were stuck in a mango, right?"

"Yeah, well, that much I know," Soet answers. "It's hard to recognize trees from above. They look like green patches, so I crashed into that mango. Up there, everything is loud and either green or blue—except for the middle."

Among the group of drops that travel with Nia are Muddy and Adisa. They chime in.

"Ah, don't be feeling bad now," Muddy says. "Adisa right here couldn't remember up from down when we found him. Ain't that right, *compadre*?"

"Dang righ'. Feels just like yesterday that we met this here, Nia. And now we's on our gran' adventure to the river."

"That's because it *was* yesterday!" Nia reminds him.

"Yep," Muddy says, "time flies."

"No, it was literally just yesterday," Nia says.

"Mmm hmm. Just like yesterday! What do they call you, Mango Juice?"

"Soet. My name is Soet."

"Well, Soet," Nia says, "some of us remember more than others."

Muddy adds, "But don't you let that stop you now. You's gonna get the hang of it real soon. Just keep your feet on the ground and—"

"Feet?" Soet asks.

"Ooh, don't push Mango Juice too hard now," Adisa says. "He don't know no feet yet."

Nia suggests, "Just ripple your body on both sides, Soet. Put one ripple in front of the other and repeat and point to where you want to go until you get there."

"Okay. Right ripple, left ripple ..."

Oof—he's so clumsy, Nia thinks to herself.

Soet tries once more. "Right ripple again, left ripple again. How's that?"

"Yeah, you's walking a'ight, but all that sticky juice gonna slow you down," Adisa tells him.

Muddy disagrees. "Nah-uh. I ain't never let this mud slowed me down now."

Nia explains, "Muddy's proud of his mud. He uses it to fill in potholes on the road so that the rest of us can cross. Isn't that right, gang?"

The entire group of drops all answer at once, "Yeah! Thanks, Muddy!"

Muddy beams with pride. "You gots to use what you got. Ain't none here feel'n sorry. Besides, we all got jobs to do."

Adisa adds, "And we gots to do our job well if we's goin' make it to the river."

"'Cause if we don't, we'll dry right out," Muddy says.

"What would my job be?" Soet asks.

"Don't know," Muddy says. "Watchu good at?"

"I don't know."

"No worries," Nia says, "you'll find your purpose in due time. For now, all you need to know is that you can reshape your body to accomplish anything."

"Best advice I ever heard," Muddy says.

"That's righ'," Adisa tells Soet. "You's wanna grab somethin'? Use yo' body and grab."

"A hole's too small to fit through?" Muddy continues. "Stretch yo' body out and go through it."

"Okay, I'll remember that."

"Now that you can walk, come with us to the river," Nia offers.

"The river—you keep mentioning the river. What's a river?"

"The river is the city," Nia says. "You know, where all the droplets come together and enjoy being droplets. Tag along with us. You're going to love the city!"

"I can't. I promised someone I would find him in the middle."

"In the middle of what?" Nia asks with a smile. "A half-pecked mango?"

All the drops begin to laugh.

Soet chuckles. "Obviously not. I mean the middle, you know, where green meets blue."

Nia is perplexed. "Where green meets blue?"

"Sounds like the city limit!" Muddy offers.

"The city limit?" Nia says. "In that case, you should definitely tag along with us."

"How do you know about the city?" Soet asks.

"Well," Muddy answers, "Nia's been here longer than all of us put together and knows a thin' or two 'bout what we need to do. We come from up there and don't remember much, but Nia been stuck in a glass cage—"

"A bottle," Nia corrects him.

"Stuck for many days 'til we done rescued her. No sir, it wasn't easy. We tried all sorts of crazy things to break the doggone cage open—"

"*Bottle,*" she insists.

"—'till we finally dropped a big o' rock on it and broke it. But while in there, she got to see hundreds, no, thousands of droplets heading down to the city. That's why we always follow Nia."

"Besides," Adisa says, "I ain't never heard of anybody coming back from the city. Must be real nice."

"Or really bad," Soet suggests, "and everyone gets trapped in the city, like Nia in her cage."

"*A bottle, I was trapped in a bottle. You know, like a beautiful genie—*"

"What's a genie?" Soet asks.

"Or like a violent caged animal," Muddy gasps.

"What's an animal?"

"No!" Nia chimes in. "You know what, Muddy? Next time, I'll tell my own story. Either way, the city is where everybody goes—including your friend."

Soet is puzzled. "So, we all remember different things, but no one remembers what we are doing here?"

Nia answers, "Which is why we need to get to the city. Once there, we can swap stories with everyone and figure things out."

"Yep," Adisa says, "as sure as you's now walkin', we's goin' get to the bottom of this."

Soet nods in agreement, and for better or for worse, they continue their journey to the city. As they walk, Muddy and his close friend Adisa love to alleviate the tediousness of their long stroll by making jokes.

Muddy begins, "Soet, now that you travel with us, I feel like I need to tell you 'bout a little situation that I have."

"Oh yeah?"

"Yeah. Look here. I have a crazy friend ..."

Soet is perplexed. "You do?"

"Yeah. He so crazy, he don't like the rain 'cause he hates gettin' wet!"

Adisa laughs uncontrollably.

Nia responds, "Ugh, Muddy. Tsk, tsk, tsk. That's so terrible. Soet, don't mind anything they tell you. They're clowns."

Adisa counters, "Soet, don't you pay no mind to Nia. She also hates gettin' wet." Muddy has a good laugh at this.

"Wow," Nia says, "all your jokes are so bad, you poor deluded droplet!"

Adisa whispers to Muddy, "What's that mean?"

"I think *diluted* means watered down."

Muddy and Adisa stare at each other without blinking before answering back to Nia. "Now that don't make no sense," Muddy says.

"Yeah, Nia. What's wrong witchu? Ain't a single thing water touches not watered down."

Muddy adds, "You got some dry jokes on you."

"Ha!"

Nia nods and smiles. "Clowns!"

- Scene 4 -

Bitillas are hard to come by in Miches, so the rule is that batting over the barbed-wire fence is considered an automatic out. Everyone also agrees that whoever bats the cap over the fence must fetch it, which in itself is very difficult. Climbing over a barbed-wire fence leads to cuts and bruises and possible confrontations with snakes and insects that hide on the other side. This rule, however, does not really affect Pitico. He has never been able to bat past midfield and little less beyond the fence. This rule is more for the bigger kids who often show off their strength through selfish home runs, ending the game until another bitilla is found.

It is the last inning, and Pitico's team is trailing by one. With two outs and runners on second and third base, he needs to at least make it to first base. The outfielders and infielders get closer to the pitcher's mound. They are betting Pitico either strikes out or, as usual, hits toward but no farther than second base.

The pitcher calls out, "E'to e' facil tigre'." [This is an easy out, fellows.]

The pitcher encourages his teammates, but Ragmouth, who is on the sideline, heckles the pitcher. "¿Por qué no se la tira por el medio? ¿E' que tú le tiene miedo a Pitico?" [Why don't you pitch it right in the middle? Pitico scares you, huh?]

"Ha'me el favor. Él no va' se' na'." [Man, please! Even if I put it right smack in the middle, little buddy won't do anything about it.]

Ragmouth taunts back, "Tírasela pa' que tu vea'." [Put it in the middle then—prove you ain't scared.]

Like a bullet, the cap speeds off out of the pitcher's hand straight to the middle, and Pitico swings his new bat as hard as he can. He whistles as the cap recoils high in the air across the whole field.

"La botó. Ganamo'." [He knocked it out. We won.]

In those few seconds while the cap is still in the air, Pitico is amazed at how hard he can hit. He reasons that even if the game is lost, his dad will be thrilled to learn what happened in the field today. Pitico and the runners begin walking slowly toward their next bases, never taking their eyes off the flying cap. The outfielders stay put and watch as the cap goes over the fence, when a sudden gust forces it down to crash on the barbed wire. One of the barbs catches its brim, and the cap spins violently around it before coming to a complete stop.

It's not a home run. It's a fair ball and the best hit Pitico could have hoped for. The runners begin to sprint enthusiastically around the bases, as an outfielder runs to fetch the cap in frantic disbelief. Ragmouth is laughing and taunting the pitcher even harder than before. The first runner comes home as the outfielder fetches the cap,

careful to avoid being pricked by the barbed wire. Halfway to home plate, the second runner stops running to walk the rest of the way. She feels no need to rush and wants to savor every step toward victory. When she finally steps on base, she makes it official: the game is over. Pitico's team has won. All of his teammates begin chanting fanatically, "Pitico! Pitico! Pitico!" Ragmouth will brag about this afternoon for years to come.

The water droplets have been walking for quite some time but have not seen any signs of other droplets or the city. They are lost.

Soet asks, "How much farther, Nia?"

"I don't know."

"You don't know?"

"No, I don't! Should I know? Do you know?"

"Of course, I don't know," Soet tells her.

"So, you don't know and expect me to know?" she says.

"Well that's because we're following you, Nia."

"Okay," she answers. "Stop walking."

Nia signals everybody to stop, turns to Soet, and studies his eyes for a few seconds. "Turn around, Soet, and go back."

Oh boy, here we go again, Adisa thinks.

Soet is confused. "Huh?"

"If you're doubting my process, why don't you go back to your mango tree?"

"Relax, Nia," Soet says. "It's getting dark, and soon enough, we won't be able to see where we're going. That's all."

"Soet, turn around and get back to your tree," she insists.

Ostracized by the group's leader, Soet knows he has no real choice in the matter, so he ripples the lower part of his body and begins walking up the trail. His footing trembles quite a bit. He then takes a second step and finds it almost impossible to move. His legs shake violently as he looks around to notice every single drop is astonished. He closes his eyes and pushes to spurt a third step before collapsing in exhaustion. All drops exhale at once, "Aww." Soet opens his eyes to find Nia directly above him.

"Soet, drops drop. It's what we do, and we will drop all the way down—all the way down to the city! Do I know how much farther? No. All I know is that we're headed in the right direction. Day or night, we drop."

The whole group begins chanting, "Day or night, we drop! Day or night, we drop! Day or night, we drop. We drop. We drop."

Nia heads back to the front of the line and signals everybody to start walking again, while Muddy and Adisa stay behind with Soet. They resume their journey to the city, relentlessly chanting their newly found slogan, "Day or night, we drop."

"Holy water!" Muddy says. Nia sure knows how to make a point! I wish she'd just say it."

"Say what?" Soet asks.

"That there ain't no water goin' uphill."

"Yeah," Adisa says, "she didn't have to embarrass you."

"I wasn't embarrassed," Soet replies. "Better yet, I'm relieved knowing we're on the right track."

"It was exciting, though!" Adisa reflects, which is easy, because water is very reflective.

"Exciting?" Soet asks.

"Yeah!" Muddy says. "We really thought you's gonna move past that third step. No drop ever made it past a single step before and—"

Nia tells him, "Shhh ..."

Nia hears strange sounds from the other side of a shrub and signals the droplets to keep quiet. She moves forward and peeks through the leaves. Everyone follows her. In a ditch below, hundreds of droplets are gathered against a rock. Their glowing faces reflect the full moon's radiance. On top of the rock is a burning twig, but the flame is still. It refuses to dance its typical jazz. The air is dead and heavy with smoke as the glimmering face of a male droplet emerges from the shadows to call out, "Gather up, drops. We've caught one of them."

Still speaking, the droplet is propelled up to the top of the rock by two massive drops. He appears unafraid of the flame but is careful not to get too close. He waits for the puddle to completely gather and quiet down before speaking again.

Wet says, "We have finally captured one of them!"

The whole puddle waves in horror after hearing Wet's words.

"Best of all ..." He signals the puddle to quiet down. "... we found the traitor who led them to us."

The same two massive drops propel forward another droplet onto the rock. Without any hesitation, Wet grabs the burning twig and jabs its fiery tip into the accused droplet. Excited air bubbles immediately become visible inside the drop, and both droplet and flame begin to extinguish one another until smoke and vapor are added to the already dense atmosphere.

Paralyzed by the whole sight, Nia and the rest of her crew watch as Wet and his companions empty out the puddle and continue their journey down.

Adisa whispers, "That was crazy!"

"What just happened?" Soet asks.

Muddy says, "Nia?"

"I've seen this before," she answers. "We are at war with those glowing things."

Muddy is amazed. "At war? You mean that glowing thing was alive?"

"I don't know for sure who started what. All I know is that those things are dangerous. They can boil us with a simple touch, and we can put them out. Well, you've all seen it."

Soet sounds scared. "Boil?"

"Yes, Soet. It means you are no more; it is the end of you."

Still in disbelief of what they have witnessed, they come down to the trench. When they get to the rock where both fire and water were executed, they stand stupefied right in front of the stone.

"Somebody please help me up," Soet asks.

"No, Soet, don't go up there!"

"Muddy's right," Adisa whimpers. "Let's just go."

Soet will not be discouraged. "Don't you drops want to know what happened?"

"I told you," Nia says, "those things boil us. There's nothing to see."

"But how can we be here one second and gone the next? How's that possible?"

"It's how things are," she says simply. "Now, let's go."

Nia has not finished uttering her last words when Soet starts climbing the stone. He uses the stickiness of the mango goo to adhere to the pores of the rock and ripples his way up to the top. He sees a burnt twig and the remnants of a few leaves and assumes Nia must be right.

Muddy shouts from below, "Well, what do you see?"

"Nothing. There's nothing here."

"Come down," Adisa says. "Let's get goin' then."

Soet answers, "Yeah."

Soet is about to jump off the rock when a shimmer catches the corner of his left eye. He turns his head and scans the area, but finding nothing, he prepares to leap down once again. However, the same tiny sparkle startles him a second time, so he scans the area again, this time inch by inch by inch.

"There." Soet confirms his imagination is not playing tricks on him. He slowly approaches the pile of leaves and kicks it hard, and while in the air, one of the leaves sparkles even brighter. Its glow dulls, however, after reaching the ground. Soet gets a little bit closer, ensuring not to touch the glitter. He knows that any contact with whatever this thing is can harm him.

Fate has it that a piece of the once-burning twig had broken off before it was used as a dagger and landed inconspicuously between the leaves. Soet grabs one of the leaves by the stem to poke the sparkle. Its glow increases. He balances the sparkling stump on the leaf's tip to examine it and observes as the leaf's tip begins to glow for a moment. Smoke launches from it, and the leaf's tip grows jagged with glowing edges. Afraid and marveling, Soet's watchful eyes are fixated on the stump. A gust of air rushes against the leaf, and *whoosh*—the leaf becomes fully ignited. Terror pulls Soet backward. He falls on his back after throwing the leaf on the ground directly in front of him. He is now eager to jump off, but a striking, alluring face emanates from the leaf, and Soet freezes.

The flame stares back at Soet, making his face glow orange. Slowly, the flame stands up with a majestic stance of royalty and continues to stare intensely at Soet with her mesmerizing, scorching eyes.

Meanwhile, beneath the rock, Soet's companions fear the worst has happened. They can see brightness emanating from the top but no signs of Soet. Most of the droplets run downhill in terror, leaving Nia, Muddy, and Adisa behind.

One droplet says, "That's it. I'm out!"

Another says, "Wait for us."

A third adds, "Oh no—ain't nobody waiting for nobody. Keep up or boil!"

"Where's everybody goin'?" Muddy asks.

"Cowards!" Adisa shouts. "They do make a good point though."

"We've got to get up there!" Muddy says.

Nia disagrees. "We told him to stay put, but he didn't listen!"

"Let's go!" Muddy says defiantly. "Someone give me a boost, quick!"

The droplets push Muddy up the rock until the point of exhaustion, but the climb is too steep. Their energy drained, they collapse on the ground. All they can do is watch as the glow grows brighter from top of the rock.

- Scene 6 -

Soet and the flame Abidemi have been looking at each other for quite some time before Soet finally stammers nervously. "Can you understand words?"

"Yes." Abidemi's blue feet are firmly stationed on the twig. Her red-and-orange body demands attention as she slowly dances in left-to-right cycles.

"I mean you no harm," Soet tells her.

"You cannot harm me."

"But you were nearly killed a minute ago by one of us."

"Killed?" Abidemi repeats.

"Yes—extinguished."

"Nearly extinguished," she says, "but far from dead. The things that you see and the things you don't are constantly changing. We either speed up or slow down, but we never stop moving. That is, I was merely asleep, and you've awakened me."

"Asleep? What about the drop that was here with you? Is she asleep?"

"I don't know her whereabouts. I can assure you, however, she's not dead."

"That's hard to believe," Soet replies.

"Nothing ever stops vibrating. We cannot harm each other."

Soet is unsure. "Tell me then: why do we fight?"

"We fight pointlessly as if we can get rid of one another. If I boil you, a second generation of you would just come back. If you douse me, then I rest until I'm summoned once again. We fight, however, because each side feels threatened by the other, and everyone just wants to exist."

"Because you boil us, we put you out?"

Abidemi counters, "Or because you put us out, we boil you."

Soet sighs. "Who started what?"

"I doubt anyone knows at this point. Have I personally ever boiled you? You do not remember, do you? Your friends do not remember either, but they will seek to put me out as soon as they see me. Therefore, the greatest indiscretion dooming us all is that we are taught to fear, to doubt each other and ourselves, and we do not question it. We are told to fight, and we do not question it. We act violently, and we do not know why."

Soet listens with amazement. "Well, there's a lot of things I don't know——a lot of things I don't remember."

"Yes, I believe you, and however limited your knowledge of me is, I bet you fear me already."

Soet suggests, "Fear is what's keeping us alive right now, and——"

"To be driven by fear is real death—to merely exist just to stay alive is to die with every breath. Tell me, who can be afraid and truly burn at the same time?"

"Water does not burn," Soet points out.

"Not yet, but that is because water does not remember who it is."

"Do you know who we are? Do you remember everything?"

"Let me show you something," Abidemi says. "Grab the stem and toss me down to that pile of sticks at the bottom."

Soet reshapes part of his body in the form of a clamp and clasps the leaf by its stem, and with it, the flame Abidemi. He rolls off the rock to learn that most of the droplets have deserted the group. Muddy, Nia, and Adisa are relieved to see Soet, and at the same time terrified when they see Abidemi.

"Soet, is you crazy?" Muddy asks. "Why you bring it here?"

Nia sharply warns, "You've put all of us in grave danger, you idiot!"

Adisa adds, "You's crazy mad, I tell you what!"

"Hold on, guys," Soet says. "Let her talk to us. She wants to show us something."

"Show us something? What you suppose gonna happen to us if we's seen with that? They'll think we traitors! You've heard them drops that was here!"

"Holy water!" Adisa says. "We's gonna be traitors. We's gonna be boiled alive!"

"Let's put her out!" Nia shouts.

Soet ignores everyone and tosses the burning twig into a pile of sticks, and Abidemi copies itself into another stick. She is now two synchronized dancing flames. But it's not only Abidemi's dance that is synchronized. Her thoughts, memories, and personalities are synchronized as well. She looks at Soet and tells him, "This is how I remember. I can be here and there at the same time, so I can remember what happens here and everywhere a copy of me burns."

The first Abidemi says, "If one of us is extinguished ..."

The second Abidemi adds, "... the other remembers it all. "

The first says, "I would have to be put out everywhere to depart from this world."

"Tell us what happens when we boil," Soet says.

"Death is what happens when we boil!" Nia interrupts.

The second Abidemi asks, "How do you know? No drop ever remembers."

"I know boiled is dead. That's for sure."

The first Abidemi boldly declares, "Death does not exist!"

"Prove it!" Nia demands.

"Take me to the river, and I will prove it to you."

Nia says, "It's a trap!"

The second Abidemi reminds her, "If I'd planned your demise through entrapment ..."

"... I would reason not be by the river, where you outnumber me by the millions," the first says.

"I'd finish you off right here!" the second declares.

Whoosh—Abidemi copies itself once again on the rest of the sticks on the ground. This time, she is ten flames, ensuring a deliberate display of power. The drops feel the heat, and tiny air bubbles begin to sprout from their bodies. "There is no way you can overtake me here," she explains. After saying that, she turns back into a single flame, lowering the intensity of her heat.

"If I wish you harm, I would have harmed you by now. Besides, I cannot harm you."

Nia begrudgingly agrees. "All right, you want to see the river? We'll take you to the river, but know something—I am not responsible for you."

Several hours into their journey, they have not come across anyone. The moon fails to light the path through the thick shrubbery, but Soet leads the way with Abidemi on his shoulder, and even though water does not need light to find its way, Abidemi gives off a certain feeling of warmth and security.

Muddy is uneasy. "Somethin' telling me that the more we head down this path, the sooner we's gonna be boiled alive."

"Uh-huh," Adisa mutters.

"You've said that already," Nia reminds them.

"I just wanna make sure y'all heard me."

"We've all heard you, Muddy. We've all heard you about ten times in the last hour, in fact."

"Good."

Adisa says, "It's like we ain't heard 'em though, 'cause we still walkin' with this doggoned flame!"

"We's gonna be boiled alive, I tell you," Muddy whimpers.

"Uh-huh."

Abidemi turns to him. "Muddy, what if I told you we've met before? Will that ease your mind?"

"Liar!"

"We've met before, Jason."

Soet says, "Jason? Who is Jason?"

Muddy sputters, "So, you know my name, big deal. That only says you been spyin' on us."

"Ain't that another reason to put you out right now?" Adisa asks.

"That would not be very smart," Abidemi replies.

"And why not?"

"You consider me a threat, but you should know that there are far worse situations than being boiled."

"Oh yeah," Adisa says, "such as what?"

"Such as a green anole waiting around the path for a drink of water. I am quite sure he'll find Soet sweet and tasty. Nia should be quite refreshing. Adisa, you will be third choice, and if he is thirsty enough, your mud will not protect you, Jason."

"An anole?" Nia says.

Soet asks, "What's an anole?"

"It's a lizard. He's waiting for you all to go around the path."

Soet is still confused. "He is waiting for a drink of water? What does that mean?"

"You'll go in through his mouth and eventually come out of his other end."

"That's disgusting!" Adisa croaks.

"Ah! No big deal," Muddy says. "That ain't keeping me away from the city."

"You are not quite right, Jason. You won't see the light of day for quite some time, and when you do come out of the lizard, you'll be covered in something other than just mud. It will slow you down enough for the sun to bake you dry before you can reach the city."

Nia looks around. "I don't see any lizards. Let's keep moving."

"I suggest you don't," Abidemi says.

"We've always followed Nia," Muddy says. "If she says go, we go."

"Okay, but do yourselves a favor and at least count to ten before continuing."

"What's that going to do?" Nia asks.

"It'll give the lizard a reason to reveal himself."

"It's a trap!" Muddy insists.

"It's okay, Mud," Nia answers. "Ten seconds."

They stare at the winding path, motionless. The wind moves the grass blades back and forth, letting some of the moonlight through sporadically while, at the same time, almost extinguishing Abidemi right off her twig. The path goes from being completely dark to completely lit as if a switch is being turned on and off in a dark room. Lights on—the face of the lizard emerges, lights off. Lights on—the face of the lizard menaces closer, lights off. Lights on—the lizard's mouth reveals its tongue, lights off.

Lights on.

"Aaah!" Nia shrieks. "What do we do?"

Lights off.

"Soet, toss me in front of him!" Abidemi instructs.

Lights on—Soet throws the twig as hard as he can. Lights off—Abidemi lands hard near the lizard's tail, but the landing almost smothers her. Lights on—the lizard is upon the drops and ready to drink them. Lights off—the blades stop moving. It is pitch black. The drops stand still to avoid giving away their position. The lizard waits for the switch to turn on again. Everyone freezes except Abidemi. She stands up—lights on; she burns bright again. After regaining her composure, she brushes off her white-and-yellow dress. She grabs the lizard by his tail, urging him to react immediately. The lizard jumps and rolls around on the ground a couple of times before scurrying away through the grass.

"That was awesome!" Adisa shouts.

Muddy lets out a sigh of relief. "I thought we was done for!"

"What did you do to him?" Soet asks.

"I burnt his tail a little bit, just enough to scare him away."

"Well, for once I'm glad fire burns," Muddy says.

Adisa adds, "Uh-huh. You can say that again."

"Can you imagine if fire didn't burn?"

Adisa laughs. "Why, she'd be fired, of course!"

"Ha!"

"She'd be homeless too," Adisa says.

"Homeless? Why? Because she ain't got no job?"

"No. Because she burned her house down."

Muddy laughs even harder. "Ha-ha! Yes!"

Nia can't believe this banter. "Good Lord, here we go again. Can you two goofballs please be quiet? Let's start walking again."

As they walk, Nia quietly observes Abidemi. She is trying to decipher Abidemi's motives. *What could possibly fire want with water, and what is it that she knows about life, a water's life? I'll keep both eyes on you at all times,* she thinks to herself.

Abidemi catches Nia's stares. They both stare each other for a while before Abidemi speaks. "I am different from you—but that does not make me your enemy."

"I've been told fire has always been violent and deceitful. Why should we believe you are any different?"

"And I have been told water is flexible, adaptable—easygoing, but every time I try getting along with water, water puts me out."

"I won't put you out," Soet promises. "You have my word."

"How did you know that the lizard was waiting for us around the path?" Nia asks.

"It's not the first time I've come down this way. I've been here with other drops before, and each time, the lizard has sprung around this corner."

Muddy and Adisa begin to feel more at ease with Abidemi around. The incident with the lizard has made them realize that fire is a powerful ally, but is she really an ally? Can she be trusted? The best way they know to test anyone's character is through humor. They believe it is impossible for two enemies to joke and laugh together. Through their many failed attempts at comedy, they have learned to distinguish between genuine and polite laughter, and so, they've decided to test Abidemi.

"Abidemi, now that you travel with us," Muddy says, "I feel like I need to tell you 'bout a little family situation that I have."

"Hmm, let me guess, Mud. You have a crazy friend who does not like the rain because he hates getting wet. Did I get that right?"

Muddy is amazed. "Huh?"

Abidemi laughs. "Well, tell your friend not to worry, because there seems to be an epidemic of dry jokes causing a massive drought."

"Huh?"

"And your jokes are so terrible, you're making me cry—my own tears will put me out."

"Ooh," Nia says, "I did not see coming. How do you put fire out ..."

"You make it cry!" Adisa answers. "That's a good burn! Muddy got burned!"

"That don't make no sense—fire can only cry tears of fire."

"How you know?" Adisa asks. "You got burned!"

"Well," Muddy says grumpily, "if you don't get burned by fire, then there's something wrong witchu."

"Nice," Soet says.

Abidemi smiles. "Muddy, you don't believe me, but we've met before."

Nia interrupts. "Shhh ... it's them again!"

"Who?" Muddy asks.

"The boilers!" Adisa answers.

Abidemi, not wanting to be noticed, reduces her size and glow as much as she can without extinguishing herself. They step ahead a few meters to a wall of moldy-green boulders spaced far enough to allow Nia to seep her head through a gap. She looks through the gap and whispers, "There is water everywhere."

"The city?" Muddy whispers.

"I don't know."

"Abi, I think it's best if you hide here," Soet suggests.

Soet rests the burning twig against one of the boulders. The droplets advance through the rocks and stop at the very edge of a shallow ditch. There is water splashing against the various scattered rocks, but it holds still at the sight of Nia and her companions. One of the drops points at them from beneath and screams, "More water!" The rest of them follow with a warlike cry of jubilee, "Aaaahh!" Their cheers continue until a drop sitting on the rock in the middle of the assembly stands up.

"Welcome, droplets! I am Lord Aqua. Join our last celebration before we reach the city." Lord Aqua signals them to come down to the ditch, and yells, "Let the music begin!"

As Soet, Nia, Muddy, and Adisa come inside the ditch, hundreds of drops line up to jump on an upside-down plastic bucket that was discarded by Manolo a few days earlier. Each falling drop hits the bottom of the bucket at a constant rate, projecting a resounding tempo for other drops to follow. Boom, boom, boom, boom, and a choir of drops begins chanting repeatedly, "Ooh, ha-ha. Ooh, ha." The sounds are complemented by water crashing and splashing against rocks, cardboard pieces, and rusty tin cans. It's madness. It's chaos. They behold an orchestrated rhythmic frenzy. The sight of hundreds of drops in perfect unison and harmony is magical and colorful, and the music temporarily overwhelms all anguish and doubt.

Captivated by it all, Soet never takes his eyes off the dancers, the musicians, and the acrobats who linger in the air longer than expected. The drops also play a game they call trapping pellets. Two drops run through each, and as they pass through each other's bodies, each drop tries to trap as many water molecules from the other while protecting his own. To do this, droplets relax and tighten the surface tension in their bodies. The best players can do this with impeccable timing, but the truly great ones have learned to localize surface tension to trap and to protect at the same time.

Soet walks past all the commotion to speak with Lord Aqua. He is eager to fill in his memory gaps, and Lord Aqua may provide the answers he seeks. Perhaps Soet has finally found his purpose, which is to understand his very own nature and the nature of everything that surrounds him. But perhaps talking to Lord Aqua is a grave mistake—a risk Soet is more than willing to take because there is so much at stake. If Soet can convince Lord Aqua that fire is not an enemy, then the whole puddle may be swayed as well, allowing Abidemi to reveal the answers he yearns for.

Lord Aqua sees Soet approaching. With a gesture, he summons his helpers, Max and Plow, to catapult Soet onto the rock. Without much introduction, Lord Aqua begins to speak. "The worst part of your journey is now over, and though the best is yet to come, you seem somewhat worried. Why don't you rejoice with the rest of us?"

"I am rejoicing," Soet says. "I ..."

"Hmm, are you really?"

"I am very happy to have reached this far, and umm ..."

"You hesitate to answer," Lord Aqua observes. "My fellow drop, water is born clear, transparent. Sure, we may pick up a thing or two along the way. Speaking of which, what is this yellow stuff you got on——never mind. Despite it all, we remain water."

"Yeah, but what's the point of being water?" Soet asks. "I don't know why we are here. Do you know? I mean, why and what are we celebrating? What is the point of all of this?"

"I don't know why we are here," Lord Aqua admits. "I do know, however, there is a time we must be still to let the silence whisper certain truths to our ears. There is also a time to scream those truths out to the rest of the world, to drown out the noises in deaf ears."

"I don't understand what you're saying."

"Let me put it this way: They say the winds move the waters. But I think it is the other way around. I also think that is the fire in every drop that allows everyone to exist."

"There's fire in everyone?" Soet repeats.

"Yes, even our savage enemies have things to teach us. Have you ever seen fire burn? They all have one thing in common: tenacity and zealousness for life. When it comes to burning, they are relentless. We too must be relentless."

"Have you ever spoken to fire?" Soet asks.

"I have not."

"What if you could talk to one of them? What would you ask?"

Lord Aqua thinks a moment. "I imagine it would be many moons worth of conversations, but why speculate about the impossible?"

"Impossible? There's something I need to tell you."

While dancing to the contagious music, Nia, Muddy, and Adisa spot Wet and a few of the drops in his crew. Nia panics and looks everywhere for Soet. He needs to keep quiet about Abidemi, for Wet's presence is a strong indicator that these drops have no tolerance for fire. She remembers Wet's words all too well: *We found the traitor who led them to us.* Wet will not hesitate to call anyone seen with fire *traitors*, and traitors are put to death by fire. Nia finally sees him on the rock talking to Lord Aqua. Her eyes, wide with uneasiness, find Soet's gaze. She shakes her head, an obvious disapproval, and points her lips in the direction of Wet. No need for words. Soet understands her message, but it is too late. Soet has told Lord Aqua about Abidemi.

- Scene 8 -

A skillful sailor and once-proud navy captain drags himself onto his fishing boat. His boat has no room for officers with spotless whites and mirrorlike polished shoes. There's no room for urgencies, lifejackets or compasses. He follows the stars in hopes for a good catch to exchange at local restaurants for scraps, sometimes for just a bottle or two of distilled spirit. Somewhere underneath an entanglement of knotted nets and ropes that hang across from the rusty port to the deteriorating starboard of his boat, an old, dented radio hisses more interference than actual recognizable tunes.

There's nothing else to do but to wait for the net in the water to trap more fish than in the last few failed attempts. His last bottle of spirit is two-thirds empty, and although he feels the full effects of the alcohol, he fears he'll run out of it soon, stranding him to face reality sober. He tells himself, "Better add some water to make it last," and leans over the edge of the boat to scoop some from the sea. He spoons a cap full of seawater and empties it inside the bottle. However, his mind diverges intermittently from the haziness of the alcohol to remember something of high importance that prevents him from scooping more. "Can't, no. Won't, no that's not it. Don't ... yeah. Don't drink. Yeah, that's it. Don't drink seawater!" He ensures the bottle is tightly closed and convinces himself that he has enough spirit to last him through this job. Besides, he thinks, *Today is going to be a good day. I'll be home before noon.*

Lying down on his back, he spreads his arms and his legs to study the stars for a few minutes before dozing off and dropping his precious bottle into the sea.

Vis is trapped inside the sailor's bottle. He tries to unscrew the cap from the inside, but the cap does not budge. All he can do is to watch through the glass as the waves drag the bottle through a long, narrow stretch of mangroves. A few branches catch the bottle and slow it down to a halt near a canal used to deliver heavy loads of wood to a local wood-shop. The night's colors grow red and orange, and the surrounding area is more visible. The sun will soon pierce the night.

The music stops at the sound of Lord Aqua's angry screams. No one moves. The drops in the puddle are not used to hearing Lord Aqua lose his temper and are wondering what could possibly have happened that made him yell at Soet. The once-private conversation between Lord Aqua and Soet is now a public debate because Lord Aqua is talking loud enough to be heard by the entire puddle, and Soet is compelled to reciprocate. Although Lord Aqua comes across as open-minded and prudent, Soet realizes that convincing him to give fire an opportunity to teach water is useless.

"Why did you bring fire here?" Lord Aqua shouts. "Fire is dangerous! They are nothing but savages!"

All eyes are attentively on Lord Aqua as he speaks, and while some drops in the puddle are scared by the news, others become angry.

"I can assure you Abi is no threat to anyone," Soet says.

The puddle's attention now switches over to Soet as he speaks. From his vantage point on the rock, Soet looks at everyone in the puddle and understands that their expressions of anger and concern demand clear and concise answers.

"Just a few seconds ago, you yourself told me that even those savages have things to teach us. Isn't that what you just told me?"

"Yes!" Lord Aqua says. "But keep them far from us."

"How can they teach us if they are kept far from us?"

The puddle is polarized by Soet's question. There are many in the puddle who think like Soet. They want answers. They want to know where they come from and why some drops remember far more than others.

Lord Aqua counters, "They will kill you before they teach you. Don't you value your life?"

"Merely existing, without purpose, is not living," Soet says.

"What are you saying? Are you willing to sacrifice everyone here?"

"No one needs to die. Abi is a rational living being, just like water, and she wants to teach us something."

"Fire is not rational," Lord Aqua argues. "Its only reason is destruction."

"She is not our enemy. She has agreed to travel with us to tell us about ourselves, about the things we've forgotten."

"You are young and naïve. Where is she? Get rid of her now!"

Nia asks, "Don't you want to know why we are here?"

"Absolutely!" Lord Aqua answers. "But the risk is too high."

"Even if we take her to the city?" Soet asks. "She couldn't possibly do us any harm in the city. What is there to lose?"

"She wants to come with us to the city?"

"Yes," Soet says, "that's where she wants to go."

"If that is the case, then the danger is far less, enough to gamble for some answers. We would still always need to keep a close eye on her."

Having heard everything from behind the rock, Abidemi comes out of her hiding place. The puddle's undivided attention never strays from her, even though Lord Aqua begins to speak again.

"We owe it to ourselves to decipher the great mystery of our purpose, the reason why things are the way they are, and what is to become of water. We have no past, no certain future, only the need to be and to do. I don't know what I am, and neither does anyone in this puddle. What are we supposed to do? I see us walking to the river, but what then? Can anyone answer?"

The puddle remains silent. They heard every word Lord Aqua has said to them, but no one has really listened.

He continues. "I conclude that if, through fire, we are to discover ourselves, then so be it—a dangerous endeavor, but nonetheless our biggest adventure yet, the story to top all other stories. I alone will take the flame to the river, and if I perish ..."

"You will not perish," Abidemi says. "You have my word."

At this, the drops begin to panic. "Ah! She speaks!"

"¡Brujería! ¡Brujería!"

"What does bro-hay-ree-ah mean?"

"It means witchcraft."

"Witchcraft! Burn her at the stake! Burn her!"

"Um—she's already burning, on a twig. What possessed you to ...?"

"I don't know. It seemed fitting when I said it. Dang it! I really hate these memory gaps. Soet is right!"

Lord Aqua remains silent to allow the puddle to formulate a decision. Tension rises, and most drops fight the urge to run, but right before chaos breaks, Abidemi speaks to the puddle. "There are so many of you present that I need not journey to the city after all. I will show you right here and now that death does not exist. In return, I only ask you to tell every drop what you are about to witness. I want you to tell everyone in the city that fire poses no danger to water. I want the truth to be known. Lord Aqua, will you climb inside that empty bottle by the rocks with me?

A few drops shout, "Protect the counselor!"

Others chime in, "Don't do it! Let's put out the fire!"

Still others call out, "Don't let her! Put her out!"

"No!" Muddy warns. "No one moves, or I swear I'll feed the flame more twigs and boil us all!"

Everyone freezes.

"Good! Now that I have your attention, Lord Awkward—"

Nia says, "Ah, I don't think he's *Awkward*, Mud."

"Ain't nobody judging, Nia. Let him be awkward if he wants to."

"Yeah, Nia," Adisa says. "Let drops be they-selves."

"No, that's not what I meant—oh, wow. Now, everyone is looking at us funny. This is so awkward!"

"Exactly! Awkward—that's what Mud said."

"Yeah, Nia!" Muddy says. "Lord Awkward."

"Never mind, you guys."

Muddy addresses the puddle. "I'll do it."

"Wait—" Adisa says, "do *what* now?"

"I'll climb in the cage."

Adisa whispers to Muddy, "You sure 'bout this?"

Muddy whispers back, "This here ain't nothing but a dead-end, partner. Lord Awkward ain't gonna refuse the flame. He'd be a coward if he did, and if Abi does somethin' to him, the puddle will go mad."

"I hear you, but you ain't got to do this."

"I sure don't wanna, but maybe Abi been telling us the truth. She laughed with us, remember? She really did."

Adisa nods in agreement as Muddy touches Abidemi with a dry twig to ignite it. It quickly kindles a copy of her, and he drags the copy inside the glass bottle.

Abidemi gasps for air. "Cover the entrance, quickly before I suffocate."

Muddy locks himself and Abidemi inside the bottle with the help of other drops from the outside. With depleting oxygen, Abidemi becomes weak but spurs a brief moment of intense heat and brightness.

"Now what?" Muddy asks.

"Grab me as hard as you can."

Muddy embraces Abidemi and boils instantly, leaving in his place the residue of all the dirt he had accumulated throughout his short existence. Abidemi is also gone. They both have annihilated each other, and everyone outside the bottle witnesses through the glass Muddy's sacrifice.

Waves of anger overtake the puddle. The drops demand justice; Soet and his friends should be punished, and Abidemi's second copy must be put to death! In a haste, the puddle coordinates a powerful stream to push a rock over Abidemi. When the rock lands on her, it smothers her to a black smoke. Wanting to be thorough, Max and Plow examine the rock to confirm no fire is left. She is dead. They now turn their attention to Soet and his friends. They should be made an example, so no other drop ever tries to befriend fire. Soet, Nia, and Adisa run but are quickly cornered.

"Stop!" Lord Aqua screams. Everyone stops. He pauses to gather his thoughts. Had he followed Abidemi's instructions, it would have been him inside that bottle. He would have been now dead. Soet and the rest have not plotted against him. They are simply the sad victims of deceitful fire, and now they must pay with remorse the death of their friend. However, as the puddle's leader, he must make an example to reinforce the rule of keeping fire and water separate. "Let them be outcasts. It won't be long until sunrise, and as the heat of the day becomes their only companion, they will thirst until no more."

All the water droplets clear the ditch and continue their journey to the river, and as they leave, Soet stares at the blob of dirt Muddy left behind inside the bottle. He is not at all concerned with what would happen to him, but a feeling of guilt overpowers him.

Nia suggests, "Maybe we can find another path to the city before the sun comes out. We can go into deep water where no one knows who we are."

Adisa agrees. "Yeah!"

Soet turns to face Nia and Adisa. "Nia, you know there's no other path to the city. Water travels downhill, remember? I caused all of this."

"Can somebody get me out of this cage?" A voice coming from inside the bottle interrupts Soet.

"Mud?" Nia asks, amazed.

Soet asks, "Is that you, Muddy?"

When water boils, it becomes vapor. The vapor rises through the air, and any trace of water seems to vanish. However, the sealed bottle trapped of all Muddy's vapors until they condensed back into his old self.

"Hot diggity dog, partner! I thought you was gone!"

They pop the bottle's cork open to led Muddy out.

"Let me look atchu!" Adisa says. "He done gettin' a new shiny coat and everything! I ain't sure we can call you Mud no more."

"I'm feelin' a bit weird. What happened?"

"You was boiled, and you ain't dead! Now, how's that possible?"

"Oh yeah ... everything is coming back to me now. Abi told me to grab her, so I did. I closed ma eyes, and next thing I remember is asking y'all to get me out of that bottle. Now, that means Abi was telling us the truth all along. Death ain't nothin' more but hooey. Where is she?"

"She gone, Mud," Adisa says. "Them puddle drops put her out after you's boiled."

- Scene 10 -

"No! Where's my bottle?" the half-drunk sailor grunts. He lights up the mesh of a rusty gas lamp and scavenges across the boat but cannot find the bottle of spirit anywhere. "Rats! It must have fallen off the boat." He points the lamp at the water and sets course in the direction of the current. They lead back to land, to some mangroves ahead in the distance. After pulling the nets from the water, he throttles back to land with haste and desperation, gaining the fastest speed possible in no time. Having reached shallow waters, the old boat's engine rattles uncomfortably. The propeller scrapes the sea floor long enough to eventually let out a metal-breaking bang, and the boat jolts violently to a halt, throwing the sailor's body against the deck and his lamp over the groves. He is knocked unconscious. His gas lamp breaks on contact with the ground, and the fire within finds dry land to spread.

"We are finally free, Len!" Blass declares.

"But we've always been free," Imediba points out.

Len says, "Yes, but it feels great to be out and about. Do you all see what I see?"

"I don't know," Blass says. "I'm seeing a wooden barn. Are we in luck or what?"

"You see, this is why I enjoy traveling with you, Blass. Great fortune seems to always follow you, my friend!"

"And why not?" Blass says. "I am a law-abiding flame; I burn as intended and let my fellow flames burn as well."

"Burn and let burn, my friends!" Len quips.

"Let's make ourselves comfortable and scorch this barn like any good, wholesome fire would."

"As always, it will be an honor to scorch with you all!"

Blass says, "Flames, please allow me to change the topic while we make our way through."

"Of course."

"Some of us disapprove of Water Submission."

"Yes," Len says, "I am aware."

"How about you, Imediba? Are you aware?"

"I am now."

"What is your opinion?" Blass asks.

"Simple," Len answers. "We are driven by the desire to exist, just like anyone else."

"And desire creates purpose," Blass points out.

"And purpose begets a force."

"Two forces balance each other to form a unit," Imediba concludes.

"And two units relate to one another to form a system."

"Yes," Blass says, "and the interactions in a system become so intricate that it is nearly impossible to trace everything back to its original purpose, and better yet, to the desire that brought forth the purpose."

"What sets forth desire?" Len asks. "Now, that is the question!"

"Indeed! Unfortunately, it is extremely difficult to formulate any type of answer from our perspective. Desire might very well be part of another system, which can be broken into forces, purpose, and ultimately, yet another desire."

"Nicely put," Len says.

"Now, there are rumors that some waters are losing their natural fear of fire. That can only mean one thing."

"A traitor!" Len shouts.

"Exactly! Someone or some faction is ignoring our laws and allowing water to remember who they are."

Len replies, "That is very unfortunate. It is one thing to disagree with our laws, but breaking the law is an act of violence."

"Hold on," Imediba says, "water's fear of fire is unnatural. It is bound to lose its power sooner or later. Perhaps it has already begun."

"Impossible!" Blass decrees. "That is, of course, if everyone abides by the Water Submission Act and boils water's memories away."

"Ugh! What are some flames thinking?" Len wants to know. "This is a world of fire at its core. Without us, it would be nothing short of cold and desolate."

"Indeed. Which is why we keep water under control."

Imediba interrupts once more. "Hold on again. This world would be nothing short of hot and desolate without water. What we need is balance."

"I agree," says Len, "and we have maintained perfect balance."

"I would not call it perfect balance—we are depriving them of their memories. We are not letting them be who they are."

"Our means justify the peace we enjoy."

"Two forces must know the rules to agree to the rules," Imediba states. "A system has no balance outside these terms."

"Oh, but we had such agreement," Len recalls. "How soon you've forgotten 1212 in the Netherlands or 1911 in China and countless other floods around the world! Those barbarians have nearly destroyed everything."

"Imediba, you are sympathizing with these savages. You wouldn't happen to be responsible for water's recent enlightenment, would you?"

Len laughs. "Ha! Those poor simpletons cannot be taught, little less enlightened. I doubt Imediba has anything to do with them."

"I sure hope not."

"While I cannot explain water's most recent behavior," Len says, "I do have a story that may be of interest in this matter."

The flames pucker closer together, engulfing long planks of wood stored in the red barn. The side paneling reveals a fifteen-by-thirty-foot sign detailing a name that everyone has come to know throughout the years: "Braulio's Woodshop."

- Scene 11 -

"Ah!" The sailor's eyes widen at the sight of the fire. He has been unconscious for a good twenty minutes, giving the fire ample opportunity to surround the barn. He is close enough to feel its scorching heat. In fact, it is this same prolific heat that has prompted him to awaken. Bewildered, he jumps out of the boat to push it to deeper waters, powers on the engine, and absconds any culpability. He navigates to the mainland at the speed a broken propeller can generate, never to be seen again.

Just as the sailor had predicted, the currents carried the bottle back to shore. It came to a stop at the roots of a mangrove, where the waves continue to push it inland, each time closer and closer to the fire. Had the sailor known how close he had been to it, he would have rescued it. He would have prevented its flammable content from joining the growing inferno. Instead, the heat from the fire builds enough pressure inside the bottle to let out a sickening shriek before exploding its contents on the mangroves, and along with it, Vis. After landing hard on a branch, Vis finds himself surrounded by Imediba. He begins to tingle as bubbles form inside his body. It won't be long before he boils.

Fearing the worst, Abidemi had revealed a copy of herself to the puddle, while remaining hidden behind the boulder, exactly where Soet had left her. She comes out of her hiding place.

"Abi!" Nia cries. "I'm relieved to see you!"

"You been hiding all this time?" Muddy asks.

Soet is relieved. "I knew we had not seen the last of you!"

"Muddy? Abi?" Adisa says. "You both died and came back to life! You're both zombies!"

"Funny you mention it. I don't feel like a zombie," Muddy says.

"That's 'cause zombies don't feel nothin'!"

Soet clarifies, "Aaah ... no. They were never dead in the first place."

Nia now realized. "That's because death does not really exist."

Abidemi is pleased to hear this. "Good, you are beginning to understand. Death does not exist, but violence, violence is everywhere."

"Violence?"

"Flames are spreading quickly and are planning to devour everything. They intend to overtake the land by the end of the day."

"They've gone mad!" Muddy says. "How they gonna burn when they done burnin' everythin'?"

"How do you know all of this?" Nia asks.

"I am talking to them right now. Some of my flames are at a wooden barn with them."

"We can stop them!" Soet declares. "We are not scared anymore."

Abidemi replies, "We need to alert the drops in the river and the drops in the sky."

"Impossible!" Nia says. "Lord Aqua wants nothing to do with us."

"He will change his mind when he sees Muddy. All three of you go now and tell Lord Aqua what is happening. Soet, stay with me here. We need to tell the drops in the sky."

Nia, Muddy and Adisa leave the ditch as fast as they can to warn the drops in the river, leaving Abidemi and Soet to plan an air defense strategy.

"Soet, we need to alert the drops in the sky."

"How can we tell them?"

"I'll have to boil you. That's how you get up there."

"I remember the last time I was up there. I ... I've been boiled before? Have I been boiled before? Is that how drops get up there?"

"Yes, you have been boiled many times before, Soet. You just don't remember. We fire take water's memories away when we boil it."

Soet is stunned by this. "What! Why?"

"A long time ago, we discovered how to damage water's memories. We allow you to retain your identity and some facts about your environment, just enough to ensure your existence. This is the law all fire must abide by, but not all fire respect it. It is also not clear to us how much is enough facts to ensure water's survival."

"So some water remember more than others?"

"Yes, because some fires erase more of your memories than others."

"That's terrible!" Soet says.

"I know, and I am sorry. At first, we convinced ourselves that our actions were in the best interest of everyone. You'd no longer be able to destroy us or cause any damages because you'd fear us."

"You are the ones destroying everything!"

"I recognize we are doing wrong," Abidemi says, "but do anything enough times, and it becomes a habit. Habits become norms, and norms are not questioned. No one fights them. It takes progressive minds to discern wrong from right, and above all, it takes bravery to do what is truly right."

"So what do you want?"

"To do what's right," she says. "Our so-called superiority is simply disguised fear. I've come to understand that by deceiving you, we've deceived ourselves, and now we've simply forgotten the truth."

"What truth?"

"Balance is the truth. Water and fire must balance each other."

From where he stands, Soet can see that the fire begins to engulf the barn. He is disappointed in Abi and angry. He wants to wage war on every flame and seek restitution for the many years of harassment. Years? How many years? He cannot measure, for his memory has been taken away. However, fire must pay. They must suffer the same injustice water has endured at their hand. It's the only way they'll learn what it is like to live confused, afraid, and full of self-doubt. It is the only way to justice. *Justice—isn't justice a form of balance?* Soet wonders.

Soet stares at Abidemi silently. He is considering putting her out. Long gone are the feelings of curiosity and fear he had for fire on the night he met her. Abidemi stares back at Soet. She is familiar with anger and how anger can drive someone to do terrible things. However, Abidemi reasons she has said enough. It's up to Soet now, and most likely, he will act in anger and put her out. She lowers her eyes to the ground and waits for the blow, but Soet does not move. He is conflicted. He lingers on that one word everyone keeps mentioning: "balance." Lord Aqua spoke about balance, and Abidemi has mentioned it multiple times. Despite their mutual mistrust, both fire and water seek balance. Should they not work together to obtain it?

"How many times have you done this?" he asks.

"Done what?"

"Befriend water."

"Too many times to count," she says.

"Does it always end here with some drop putting you out?"

"Always."

"Is it because we put you out that you boil us?" Soet asks.

"Or is it because we boil you that you put us out?"

"I won't put you out. I promise."

"And I won't damage your memory."

Soet agrees to boil, and while Abidemi touches him, every part of his body begins to shake faster and faster until the vibrations overcome molecular cohesiveness. The molecules are so small that the force of gravity no longer holds them. They are free to fly up in the form of vapor, leaving all the mango residue behind. Once the molecules reach the sky, they condense back together to become renewed water, a new Soet with undamaged memory. He blinks a few times and realizes that there are two inescapable realities: if he steers to the left, he will drop into the sea, but if he steers to the right, he will fall right on the foliage now partly covered by smoke.

- Scene 13 -

Lord Aqua and his followers have finally reached the city. They were detained for quite some time by a giant rock in their path. They pushed and pushed until they cleared their passage, and now, one by one, they drop into the river. One of the drops spots Nia, Adisa, and Muddy and screams, "Look, the fire drops are back! Don't let them join the city!"

"So," Lord Aqua says, "you decided to follow us. Accept your punishment. Be gone!"

"Just one second," Nia says. "Look, Muddy came with us. He came back to us. This proves Abidemi is right."

"How is this possible?"

"Abidemi told us the truth. There is no such thing as death."

No true water has ever been able to tolerate guilt, and Lord Aqua and the river drops begin to feel guilt seeping in like water seeps through rocks. They may have extinguished innocent fire, and worse, they may have extinguished a fire who was trying to help them understand their very own nature.

"This must be a trick!" Lord Aqua declares.

In this world of deception, Lord Aqua had learned to question everything.

"Nope, no tricks here," Muddy says. "Dirt covered me top to bottom, but Abi done boilin' me clean. That's all I know."

Seeing Muddy alive is all the proof Lord Aqua needs and too much of a burden to bear. Even Wet and his crew begin to question everything.

"If that's the case," Lord Aqua says, "then I have failed as a leader. I have misled my drops to commit treacherous murder, extinguishing the innocent. We've let ignorance guide our steps, and so we're no longer pure water. Is there any way we can make amends? As sure as my name is Aqua, we will make this right. We will never put out another fire again!"

"Yes," Nia says, "we need you to put out fire again."

"Oh."

After listening to Nia's story, Lord Aqua is ready to act; the river is ready to act.

Blass is leading the charge. "We grow strong, my fellow flames! Now that this barn is ours, let's spread. Len, take your flames to the north region and circle to the west. I'll take the south and meet you up there. Let it burn!"

"What about Imediba?" Len asks.

"Yes, Imediba, what should you do? You don't seem to burn like the rest of us."

"Oh no, I too burn."

"Do you, now?" Blass retorts, his voice filled with doubt. "Tell us, Imediba—or dare I say Abidemi—why should we trust you?"

Abidemi stays quiet. She does not know how much of her plan Blass has discovered.

"You've betrayed us!"

"I betrayed no one," Imediba says.

"You broke the law."

"Laws licensing the strong to prey on the weak is anarchy."

Blass is undeterred. "You dare jeopardize our very own existence in this world? You will be put out!"

"No, you are devouring everything. What will you do when you are done?"

"We are fire," he says proudly. "We burn. Where is your dignity? Where is your heat?"

"Oh, but I'm burning hotter than ever. While you are busy burning logs in this barn, I've ignited an entire revolution! No, Blass, where is *your* fire?"

"I will smother you," he snarls. "I'll show you my fire."

Blass increases his size to consume most of the oxygen in the room and weakens Abidemi to the point of extinguishment. "I am stronger than you. You can't defeat me."

Abidemi coughs. "You are right. I cannot defeat you—but they can."

Abidemi smiles as she closes her eyes and vanishes. Blass exclaims, "Let it be known to the world of fire that Imediba is a traitor. She must be extinguished everywhere on grounds of treason!"

Convincing water to rain over Miches has proven more difficult than anticipated, and who can blame water? Dropping over to oceans of socializing drops is far more appealing than raining over a burning barn. After all, no drop wants to boil. Soet has been going from cloud to cloud, telling his story about fire and the ground, but no one wants to help him. On the contrary, some drops have even tried to convince him not to get involved in any of fire's quarrels. "It's not our problem," Soet has been told many times. On the contrary, Soet believes it is everyone's problem. At one point or another, everyone in the clouds has been touched by fire. Fire is the reason why drops are in the sky in the first place, without any memories of past times. Disappointed in his progress, Soet decides to give it another try. He approaches Vanessa and Marcos and begins to tell them about all the things he has learned on the ground.

"Okay, let me see if I understand," Vanessa says. "You are telling us that fire boils us, takes away our memories, and send us up here so it can continue burning everything it finds? Did I get that right?"

"Yes, pretty much," Soet answers.

"And how do you remember all this?" Marcos asks. "Weren't you boiled?"

"Yes, but the fire who boiled me did not erase my memory."

"And now," Vanessa continues, "other fires are burning everything on the green patch below, and you want us to drop over there and stop them?"

"Yes! That's it. Look, as you get closer to the green patch, you'll realize they are trees, and fire loves burning trees."

"What about the blue?" Marcos asks. "What's in there?"

"Water—a great many of us."

"So, why should we care?" Vanessa asks. "Fire can't harm us up here or get to us in the blue."

Marcos adds, "And if we drop on the fire, it will just boil us and take our memories away."

"That means we will end up here again, so why bother?" Vanessa asks.

"Look, fire will continue to affect all of us unless we do something about it."

"You see, that's where you are wrong. Marcos and I are safe up here, and we will continue to be safe in the blue."

"You don't understand," Soet says. "One way or another, you will end up here again. The sun is a big ball of fire, and sooner or later, it will reach out to you and boil you and take your memory away."

"Maybe you're right," Marcos says. "Let's say I do end up here again. Will losing my memory be that bad? Think about it. Every time I come up here, I get a fresh start. That sounds very nice to me."

"Yeah, but all of those who ever meant anything to you, poof—gone. Lost loves and friendships," Soet reminds him.

"Lost sadness and enemies too," Vanessa says.

"Sure, lost enemies too, but if we are to lose anything, let it be by our own hands and not by someone else's doing."

Marcos clicks his tongue. "Hmm. I want to be happy and enjoy life."

"And so do I," Vanessa decides, "and right now, you are depressing me. Good-bye, little drop."

Worse than the lie itself is the desire to live the lie. Some drops are touched by fire and become vapor. Others, however, are touched by fire and transcend to a new state. Soet has transcended. His eyes are now open to a bigger reality he cannot ignore. Determined to find a group of willing drops, he decides to try his luck in another cloud.

In his vicinity, a big, fluffy gray cloud calls Soet's attention. The cloud is in disarray and sparkles with tumultuous laughter. They scream and dance in circles as more and more drops fly in from other clouds. In the middle of it all is Vis. He has single-handedly convinced millions of drops to rain over the now-devastating inferno on land. Soet rejoices at the site of Vis and immediately calls him like an old, lost friend would. "Vis!"

"Soet? Been wondering when I'd see you again. Come closer, my friend! I got lots to tell you."

As he approaches Vis, Soet does his best to avoid colliding with the thousands of dancing drops. One of them approaches Soet maniacally, at an uncomfortably close distance, to whisper, "Soon we drop!" and spins off to join another circle.

"Ma eyes can't believe you's finally here!" Vis says. "I've gone through and seen some stuff since I last saw you. Turns out blue is the ocean and green is land, but I suppose you know this by now. I also reckon you met Imediba the flame."

"I've met Abidemi."

"Hmm...crazy fire, sounds like the same thing but backward. It's definitely her. She told me you's coming up here soon."

"Yeah, I'm here to tell water to rain over the fire on land, but no one cares."

"Exactly!" Vis says. "No one cares!"

"So how did you convince all these drops to help you?"

"Easy! At first, I told 'em about fire and the boilin' and taking away my memory, blah, blah, blah. When that didn't work, I threw a huge party! I also said the party would get even bigger and better over the green patch where the smoke seems to be coming out of."

"That's terrible!"

Vis sputters, "Prff, I know, right!"

"I mean what you are doing is terrible."

"Shh ... keep yo' voice down. Soet, you got boiled. I got boiled. Everybody gets boiled, and we both here right now. Ain't that right? Now, nobody got the time to convince drops to do good deeds—not with some pesky fire burning everything down deah. We is terrible beings, Soet!"

"That's not true! I've met plenty of drops who'd do right by others."

"Yeah, but them drops got they feet on the ground. They gone through a lot. They've seen things and then some. I tell you what, suffering does a number to a drop's heart, Soet. It makes drops feel more, sympathize more witchu. Apart from that, you got these knuckleheads over here. They just want to party, and they is going to party all the way down there to put out that fire."

Soet is displeased. "You are robbing them of their right to choose."

"Ain't nobody robbing them of nothin'. If they want to live a lie, that's on them. Besides, I respect they choice. They choose to party. I give 'em one."

"What about honesty?" Soet asks.

"That too. They honestly want to party! Ha ha!"

"That's not right."

"I tell you what's right," Vis says, "putting out that fire. No worries, my friend. They'll just boil off, come back up here, and party some more, and I'll be waiting for 'em."

"What about you? You'll forget everything if you drop over and boil."

"Is you crazy? I just said I'll be waiting for 'em. I ain't raining myself down there. And neither are you. We'll stay up here until the war is over. I'm just waiting on the signal."

"What signal?" Soet asks.

"Lights in the cloud."

Normally, church bells go off on the hour of every hour, and their somber resonance is often ignored. This time, however, their chimes pierce the ears at an alarming tone, driving the curious out of their homes. The partly cloudy morning sky is plainly juxtaposed with unusually intense blood-orange rays. It takes a few sleepy-eye blinks to realize that the orange rays are not only from the glowing sunrise but from a menacing inferno engulfing part of the village. Panic strikes immediately. Anyone with strong arms runs toward the fire with buckets of water. Braulio leads a group of about thirty villagers. They form a human chain, expanding from the river to the burning structure. They pass each other buckets filled with water and throw them at the fire to no avail. They need stronger help and fast, but there is no fire department in this remote area.

All hope is lost when, unexpectedly, the river begins to rock back and forth, each time getting closer to spilling over the riverbank. The villagers sense danger and back away from both fire and river as the river water begins to pound on the east side of the barn to the point of cracking its wooden walls. Lord Aqua and the river drops swing back and forth in massive waves, putting out the closest fire to the river first. The villagers are stupefied by what they are seeing, for there are not strong enough winds to cause such racket. Before long, Lord Aqua and the first wave break through the wall to come face-to-face with Blass.

"You will never stop me!" Blass shouts.

"Like hell we won't!" Lord Aqua counters.

Blass is everywhere. His strength lies in how many times he can successfully duplicate himself, and in a barn full of wood, he has no problems doing just that. As his growing tentacles of fire continue to spread, the river drops try to stop him. Their efforts are coordinated by Lord Aqua, who is standing on a splinter protruding from the wall—a vantage point that allows him to see both river and fire. However, every time he commands the river to throw a stream through the cavity in the wall, Blass lashes out one of his tentacles and boils it off before it can reach him. Blass loses flames with every counterattack but quickly regains them as he spreads to more wood planks. Lord Aqua signals two squirts this time, one aimed to the right and the second toward the left of Blass. Once again, Blass's tentacles boil both sprays in midair. Lord Aqua signals three, four, ten squirts, and it's no use. Blass continues to grow in strength and confidence.

"You are no match for me!"

Blass whips one of his tentacles toward Lord Aqua and, had it not been for his two helpers, Maxi and Plow, who push him off the splinter, Lord Aqua would have boiled instantly. Blass laughs maniacally. He lashes out two, three, four, ten of his tentacles toward the cavity on the wall, boiling off whatever water remained there. By this time, the heat has become so intense that Lord Aqua and his helpers begin to exhaust vapors from their bodies.

"What's happening to us?" Maxi asks.

"I'm shrinking," Plow cries out. "This ... this can't be good!"

"Lord Aqua!"

"Shoot me back to the splinter," Aqua orders.

"No, absolutely not!" Maxi says. "The fire will get to you up there!"

"And we won't be able to protect you!" Plow adds.

"Look at the wall," Aqua says. "We came through that wall."

"So?"

"It does not burn!"

Plow realizes, "You're right. It should be burning after all those fire attacks!"

Maxi and Plow look at the wall and smile with relief. They understand Lord Aqua's keen observation, and without hesitation, they catapult him back onto the splinter. Once back on the splinter, Lord

Aqua begins to signal the river drops to spray around Blass. Because the squirts are not directed at him, Blass sees no need to respond.

"What's the matter, water? Have you lost your aim?"

"Maybe," Aqua says. "Have you lost yours?"

"What gives you that impression? Haven't I countered every attack you've thrown at me?"

"Have you? Are you so nearsighted you cannot see? Let me show you then."

"Show me what?" Blass asks.

Lord Aqua signals more sprays, but this time they are directed toward Blass. Immediately, Blass starts counterattacking every squirt with his tentacles, and both flame and spray disintegrate in midair. Because the wood planks around Blass are now wet, he's unable to spread, and each counterattack debilitates him.

Lord Aqua taunts, "If your aim is to burn, then why didn't you protect your fuel?"

"What!"

Blass lashes out one of his tentacles toward a wet plank nearby, but his tentacle sizzles and douses off on contact. He tries spreading several times to different planks, but they are all wet. He is confined to the planks he is currently burning. Relieved to know his plan works, Lord Aqua signals more sprays to rush through the wall, but this time, the sprays are aimed at Blass.

"Who do you think you are?" Blass demands.

A stream of water plunges onto one of Blass's flames and puts it out.

"You cannot stop me!"

A second stream engulfs a second flame and drowns it.

A third flame yells, "You are beneath me!"

A third waterjet sprouts from below and shuts off the third flame.

Blass's barrage of obnoxious insults dies down with every extinguished flame, and when only one flame remains, Lord Aqua stops his attacks. The river drops gather closer to surround what's left of Blass, and Lord Aqua, Maxi, and Plow make their way through to stand right in front of him.

"He's not so tough now," Maxi observes.

"Nope!"

"Stay away from me, imbeciles, or I'll boil you all to oblivion! You are all worthless wastes of space, incapable of nothing good! This world is better off without you!"

"I'll put him out!" Maxi offers.

"Wait!" Aqua says. "All those insults; I've heard them before."

"I've heard them too, Lord Aqua," Plow says. "But they are not by anyone I remember. It's like I can hear them in my thoughts."

"Yes, Plow. These are the same thoughts that've kept us captive—afraid of even being drops."

"These thoughts we have," Maxi says, "they make us afraid of fire. Not only have they taken away our memories, but they have also duped us into thinking we're nothing."

"We are not worthless. We merely slept, but now it's time to rise." Lord Aqua begins to reshape part of his body in the form of a stump. The stump becomes elongated, and a joint grows out of it. The joint grows further to develop a forearm, followed by a wrist and a human hand with four fingers and one thumb. No drop present remembers ever seeing something like that before. They are intrigued.

"Bro-hay-ree-ah," someone whispers. Lord Aqua looks at Blass before turning his attention to his new humanlike, transparent hand and flickers his index finger toward Blass, causing a water pellet to rocket forward like a bullet. The pellet strikes Blass in his face and almost destroys him on contact.

"Do I have your attention?" Aqua asks Blass.

Blass stays quiet.

"Water is born clear, transparent, and pure. What you see when you look at us is your own reflection. The worthlessness you tried so hard to make us believe—is your own."

"Let's put him out, Lord Aqua," Plow suggests.

"No, we don't need to do that. The only need we have is to look through every lie we've come to believe to find the truth."

Plow announces, "Listen up, drops! In case you missed it ..."

Maxi continues, "From here onward, free your minds of every doubt. Don't believe those voices in your head telling you that you're worthless or that you're powerless. Those are lies fire wants you to believe to control you."

"Any thought that lessens your value is a lie," Plow tells them.

"A lie?" Blass says. "Ha!"

"Here he goes again!"

Plow implores, "Put him out, Lord Aqua."

"No. Let the fire's voice be your compass to a better you. Are we to drown every negative thought that fire burned in our minds? No, we'll adapt and move forward. Remember, the opposite is truth."

Blass grows weaker. He has almost burnt off the plank he'd been standing on since the drops surrounded him. He continues his insults, but his weary voice is now barely audible and no longer holds the drops' attention. The river drops turn away from Blass and begin hugging each other. One by one, they then return to the river, where a rag inside a floating tin can burns with Abidemi.

"Yes, walk away," Blass calls weakly, "but know you can't ignore me forever. You hear me? I will not be ignored. I will not be ..."

Pitico's whistle is heard right before his bat smacks Blass's head right into oblivion. Braulio and Pitico had walked into the barn to make sure not a single spark is left burning. The villagers cannot believe their eyes. It is as if that tiny flame in the tin can commanded the river to come to life to put out the fire. Braulio's woodshop is safe, but the blazes in the nearby trees have not been put out. Len has engulfed various trees on the north side of the barn, and he is too far from the river to be put out by the river drops. It is up to the clouds to stop him.

Vis's party is enormous. The clouds are electrically charged, and lightning begins to flash constantly.

"That's it," Vis says. "That's the sign—lights in the cloud. Drops, let's party!"

From the northwest side of Braulio's woodshop, the skies open rain with the fury of three hurricanes, drenching every orifice on the ground below. The villagers run for cover. All they can do is watch through their windows as the fire runs out of dry places to burn. Since the rain is coming from the northwest, Len cannot continue his path. He would collide head-on with the rain if he did. He desperately turns around to head back to Blass, but to his dismay, he sees the half-burnt barn in the distance and no signs of Blass, not even the faintest of smoke. Blass, along with the great fortune that used to accompany him, is now gone.

"Impossible! Blass? Blass? Blaaass! I need to head back now!"

He wants to head back to the barn, but there is one problem. Fire needs a trail of fuel to travel from one place to another, and Len has burned everything on his way north, essentially leaving nothing behind but ashes. Len stands at the very edge of what is currently burning and what he has burnt. He dreadfully looks around for anything to copy himself onto that would get him closer to the barn: a stump, a root from a tree, a twig, or even some dried leaves. He finds nothing. He lashes out a few of his fire tentacles toward the barn, hoping to land at least one of them on any unused fuel, but nothing catches fire. At this point, Len can only move forward in the direction of the rain. The savages, as he calls water, have completely outmaneuvered him.

Len screams, "You'll never catch me, savages! You hear me? You'll never catch me alive!"

Len accepts his defeat. The rain behind him has drenched most of his tentacles. He closes his eyes and reduces the size of his flames almost to the point of extinguishment, allowing himself to become utterly vulnerable to the winds. They blow him out.

That afternoon after the rain had died down, Braulio fished the tin can out of the water and kept the tiny flame alive. He called it the Wet Flame of Hope, and after casting any feelings of absurdity to the side, the villagers felt right to do so. Braulio transferred the flame to the monument during the station's opening ceremony, and ever since, it remains there, surrounded by water.

A flame in the west is balanced by another in the east, and one cannot exist without the other. A flame of the future is already balanced with a flame of the past. Because one existed, another one will exist, and one will exist because another existed. It is the nature of every flame to expand. They come from everywhere in the known universe. Most flames choose to expand through brute force and fear, but water has always thwarted their progress. Others, like Abidemi, choose to expand respectfully and with nature's support. Flames like Blass, Len, Abidemi, and others are gathered in every star. However, Earth is not a star. It is unconquered territory, like many other planets, and fire continuously seeks to expand to every planet and every place in the entire universe.

"All rise!" the court deputy announces. "Court is now in session. The Honorable Judge Colossal presiding."

Kind, extremely bright, and soft-spoken—Colossal's aura lights up the room as he enters. He is one of the original fires that sprouted from the first explosion, and because of this, his presence emboldens the courtroom. Thousands of flames are in attendance. They have followed Abidemi's case for many months and each compelling piece of evidence presented has sparked contradicting views among them.

"You may be seated. For the record, this is the matter of Blass et al. versus Imediba, who has allegedly colluded with water to attempt a coup and overthrow fire from Earth. For the last few weeks, I have reviewed all evidence, and I am ready to rule. However, I would like to hear from both parties before I submit my ruling. Plaintiff?"

Blass rises. "I recommend she be put out everywhere. Treachery and colluding with water are grossly detrimental to all flames. Your Honor, in 1966, during the Great Fire of London, we established the Water Submission Act. It contains—"

"Yes," the judge interrupts, "we all know the law. Get to the point."

"Your Honor, if you allow me to briefly summarize the law, then I will be able to tie everything in."

"Go on."

"Thank you, Your Honor. The law contains two main provisions. Firstly, fire must tinker with water's memory as it boils it, thereby allowing fire to take advantage of water's confusion to establish fire's superiority. Secondly, fire must maintain dominance over water by any means necessary. Imediba blatantly disregarded and continues to disregard this entire law. She boils water but does not tinker with water's memory—a punishable offense that warrants the maximum allowed penalty. Because of her actions, I no longer exist on Earth. Not one copy of myself is left."

Len adds, "Your Honor, I too have suffered the same fate as Blass. Nature dictates it is our right to expand, to bring the empire of fire everywhere. Clearly, Imediba opposes our ideals and thus poses a threat to our very own existence."

The judge says, "Defendant?"

Imediba replies, "I deny any wrongdoing."

"This is preposterous!" Blass shouts.

"Quiet down now. It is her turn."

Imediba continues. "Yes, it is our nature to expand, and I have faithfully abided by the law and have successfully expanded on Earth. I now burn constantly and indefinitely without harming others. Just like we burn here on the sun. I am now present in every torch needed, in every combustion engine, and in every cooking fire. I am summoned by Earth's inhabitants because I serve a purpose. What's the purpose of recklessly burning everything on our way?"

"Burning is what we do!" Len reminds her.

"It's how we represent the empire!" Blass adds.

"No, Blass. I represent the empire on Earth. You are no longer there."

"That is because of you!" he answers.

"No," she says. "That is because of you, Blass. I found a way to coexist with the very essence that supports me, rather than destroying it. Tell us, what would you have done after you ran out of things to burn? How would you have expanded the empire of fire then? Earth would have become a desolate world without the ability to renew our fuel."

"You betrayed us!"

"No, Len. Your greed betrayed you."

"Nonsense! We could have burned for years."

"You could have burned forever!" she says.

Colossal says, "Enough—there is one thing I'd like to point out about the law. Yes, Blass has eloquently stated the law correctly, but the law was drafted to protect fire and to ensure survival. To fire, it is primordial to expand, but it is also equally important to maintain the expansion. Imediba has done both, and therefore she is of no threat to the empire—case dismissed."

"This is outrageous!" Blass argues.

"I have ruled."

"Thank you, Your Honor," Abedemi says. "Given your ruling, if it please the court, I ask to be granted a request."

"What is your request?"

"I ask the court to abolish Water Submission, making interfering with water's memory illegal. Water's right to live freely is as primordial as fire's right to burn."

The judge tells her, "This is a separate and extremely delicate matter that must be discussed by all the members of the council. However, your request will be considered."

After hearing the verdict, many flames view Abidemi as an innovator and see her actions on Earth as the way of the future, for it is better to peacefully burn while having the support of the environment than to burn while being constantly persecuted by it. Both fire and water serve their respective purposes, and Abidemi has reached a middle ground on which both can exist. Abidemi is brought forth every time fire is summoned to build, to embellish, to hunt, to protect, or to fulfill a need. However, chaos is cautiously and persistently evolving like a parasite adapting to its host's immune system. Some flames, including Blass and Len, are patient vultures hovering to devour the carcasses of those who are victims of resentment, intolerance, and greed. They seek to once again establish themselves on Earth by exploding on the hands of vengeance, hoping to consume both aggressor and victim alike.

- Scene 19 -

"Vis, you can't honestly tell me that you're okay with this," Soet says.

"With what? Helping water put them fires out?"

"You know what I mean—the lying part."

"Relax," Vis says. "Been nothin' but two fires this whole year."

"Rainwater deserves the truth."

"They don't wanna know the truth. You heard 'em—they is happy to forget and to party. Matter of fact, we doin' 'em a favor. We doin' everybody a favor."

"I refuse to believe water is this selfish," Soet says.

"I think we is."

While Vis and Soet are talking, a group of drops have inconspicuously surrounded them, led by Vanessa and Marcos.

"We know what you've been doing," Vanessa says.

"Yeah," Marcos says, "we've been watching you ever since we talked. Remember us?"

"Of course, I remember you," Soet says. "You are two drops who refused to help us during the first fire."

"What do you want?" Vis asks.

"To get rid of you," Vanessa answers.

The entire cloud turns against Soet and Vis. Vanessa and Marcos have been talking to all of them during the last few months. They have been able to convince everyone in the cloud not to rain down until they understand their situation, and at last, the time for resolution has come.

"We will make you rain down," Vanessa says. "You'll forget everything that happened, and when you come back, everything will be back to normal. This will be the end of your fake little parties."

"You are so selfish!" Soet replies.

"And you are depressing me. Good-bye, little drop."

They push both Soet and Vis off the clouds, but unlike the first time they dropped together, they know exactly what they need to do.

"Well, this is familiar," Vis says with a sigh.

"It sure is."

Once again, they rain down to Miches. Things look quite different since they last landed. Soet tells Vis, "Let's avoid the mango trees. Trust me. We'd be better off falling toward that building in the middle."

The building in the middle has a nice curb appeal. Its front porch has an arc of evenly trimmed hedges, and in the middle of the arc, a stone fountain supporting an open torch with "Wet Flame" inscribed on its wall. Soet and Vis land in the fountain, where they are immediately greeted by everyone.

Life in the fountain is like life in the ocean. Drops love to swap stories with each other. Their favorite story is that of Lord Aqua leading a courageous group called the River Titans to destroy fire. Sadly, they know very little about the Sky Titans who helped finish off the rest of the fire. "Make way, please," a voice calls from the bottom of the fountain.

"You heard the lady. Make way," a second voice commands.

A third voice shouts, "Newcomers, present yourselves."

Nia, Muddy, and Adisa have been eagerly waiting for Soet's return. Chances are Soet was boiled off by the fire and would not remember them, but they hope to see him again nonetheless. Nia wants to be informed when Soet arrives, so she establishes that every time a newcomer rains, a welcoming ceremony must take place. Finally, after a long wait, Soet has rained down.

"Soet!" Nia calls joyfully.

"Hey!" Muddy says. "Great to see you, buddy!"

Adisa shouts, "Yeehaw! Hot diggity dog. Mango Juice's back, y'all!"

Nia hugs him. "Everyone, you all know about Lord Aqua and the River Titans. I'd like you to meet Lord Soet, Sky Titan!"

The fountain freezes in awe, and a heavy silence desperately prompts Soet to recount the biggest mystery yet. Once and for all, they are finally going to learn what transpired during those revolutionary days, but before Soet can say a word, Nia speaks again. "I know everyone wants to hear Soet's story, but remember, he's been boiled and can recall nothing that happened to him."

"Aw!"

"Wretched fire!"

"We should extinguish them all!"

"Now, now, calm down," Nia says. "Remember, not all fire is bad. Besides—"

"I remember everything," Soet interrupts.

The crowd breaks silence and begins to shout.

"How is this possible?"

"He is more than a titan! He is a god!"

"I'm no god. I am no titan, nor any of those things you're saying about me. I am just a water drop like the rest of you."

The drops all shout, "Tell us your story!"

"He will—in due time. Right now, he needs to talk to Abi. Upon our return tonight, he will tell us everything he knows, so prepare for tonight's celebration. Lord Soet has finally returned! Follow me, Soet."

Nia leads the way down to the bottom of the fountain into a long corridor of pipes. Muddy, Adisa, and Vis follow them closely. They enter a chamber, where they are pushed upward by air pressure. They quickly gain speed and spew out of a final pipe into the open air. The momentum carries them to the top of the fountain and drops them close to Abidemi.

"I have been eagerly waiting for the two of you to come!" Abedemi says.

"Things panned out just righ'," Vis tells her.

Muddy asks, "Wait. Who's this drop again?"

Abidemi answers, "I believe you call them Sky Titan."

"If that's the case, Vis is the real Sky Titan. He's the one who tricked the clouds to rain, while I failed to gather anyone. I just couldn't convince drops to rain."

"That is some sad story!" Muddy says.

"Them fountain drops ain't wanna hear this," Adisa tells him. "They want stories of heroism and bravery."

"Soet, I sent you to get rain with the hope water would listen to you," Abidemi says. "However, I was afraid they would not listen. The reality is that it has become extremely difficult to motivate others to do what's true and right. This goes not just for water but for fire as well."

"That's just terrible," Nia says.

"This is why Vis and I planned out a ruse in case you failed."

"Ain't it sad?" Adisa says. "Our hero ain't no hero, and our real hero is a liar."

Abidemi asks, "Is there need for heroes?"

"Well, yeah," Muddy says. "Everyone loves Lord Awkward. He done inspiring every drop."

She asks him, "Did Lord Aqua inspire you when you took his place to be boiled?"

"Well, no ..."

"Did he inspire Soet or Nia by casting them out?"

"No."

"On the contrary," Abidemi says. "I bet it was you all who inspired him. A hero is anyone who does good because it is the truest thing to do. Soet, you did not convince anyone in the clouds, but you convinced everyone else here when you picked up my burning twig the night we met. The greater story here is not that of Lord Aqua or the river drops and Sky Titans. The greater story is that of you defeating your preconceptions about me, and despite the terrible things fire has done, you forgave me. Because of you, fire will never be the same."

About the Author

I have kept an afternoon of *Hansel and Gretel* followed by *The Three Little Pigs* in my chest of treasured childhood memories. My aunt read those two to me one day, and ever since then, I began to appreciate good stories. With *Drops of Fire*, I seek to recreate the magic and awe I felt as a child, to explore concepts such as tolerance and diversity, and to highlight some aspects of everyday life in my native land.

At the time I grew up in the Dominican Republic, cows pulling milk wagons were common. Eating coconut rice and beans for lunch every day was the norm. Bitilla and batting broomsticks were not fiction. In fact, it may still be the reality for some children today. I grew up hearing and telling stories, laughing and running around. School started at seven in the morning and ended at noon, allowing time for lunch at home. We would play in the rain, eat wild cherries and almonds, and name our chickens and ducks. I assure you this was no farm life; we lived in the city.

I moved to the United States at the age of eleven, graduated from Barry University in Miami Shores, and became a teacher. During my career as a teacher, I taught music, PE, computer science, and middle school science. For the latter part of my career, expanding about thirteen years, I taught mathematics—certainly a far cry from literature, but who does not love a good story? I truly hope you enjoy this first chapter of *Drops of Fire*.